P9-BYR-198

J MIL
35248001407786
24y   FEB   '10
Millard, Glenda.
The naming of Tishkin Silk

OAK CREEK (WIS.) PUBLIC LIBRARY

The Naming of
Tishkin
Silk

The Naming of
Tishkin
Silk

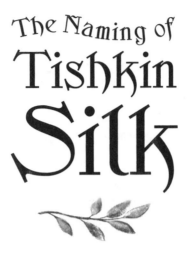

Glenda Millard

Illustrated by
Patrice Barton

OAK CREEK (WIS.) PUBLIC LIBRARY

Farrar, Straus and Giroux
New York

Text copyright © 2003 by Glenda Millard
Pictures copyright © 2009 by Patrice Barton
All rights reserved
Originally published in Australia by ABC Books
Distributed in Canada by Douglas & McIntyre Ltd.
Printed in July 2009 in the United States of America
by RR Donnelley, Bloomsburg, Pennsylvania
Designed by Irene Metaxatos
First American edition, 2009
1   3   5   7   9   10   8   6   4   2

www.fsgkidsbooks.com

Library of Congress Cataloging-in-Publication Data
Millard, Glenda.
    The naming of Tishkin Silk / Glenda Millard ; illustrated by Patrice
Barton.— 1st American ed.
        p.   cm.
    Summary: Griffin Silk feels responsible for the absence of his mother and
baby sister, but he and his new friend Layla find the perfect way to make
everyone feel a little bit better.
    ISBN: 978-0-374-35481-7
    [1. Names—Fiction.   2. Family—Fiction.   3. Death—Fiction.
4. Friendship—Fiction.   5. Self-acceptance—Fiction.   6. Australia—
Fiction.]   I. Barton, Patrice, 1955– ill.   II. Title.

PZ7.M6033Nam 2009
[Fic]—dc22

                                                    2008016796

In remembrance of lost angels

—G.M.

For Jerry

—P.B.

Contents

The Naming of
Tishkin
Silk

An Uncommon
Boy

Griffin came into the Silk family after Scarlet, Indigo, Violet, Amber, and Saffron. He came early in the morning on that uncommon day, the twenty-ninth of February. His father's prediction, considering the date of Griffin's birth, was that he would be an uncommon sort of boy.

Perhaps he was, thought Griffin ruefully. For the first time in his life, he wished he'd been born on the twenty-eighth day of February, or even the first of March. Maybe then he would have been an ordinary boy instead. If he were an ordinary boy, maybe Mama wouldn't have gone away. Maybe his secret thoughts wouldn't have changed everything.

Griffin had never felt his uncommonness until the day he started school, and it was only because the other children had made him aware of it. He wouldn't have minded being uncommon if only he could have stayed at home to learn with Mama, like his older sisters had.

It wasn't fair.

Mama had taught him well. The school principal said he was ahead of other students his age and put him into Miss Beaumont's third-grade class, where all the children were older than he was. Some of them sniggered to each other behind cupped hands when the teacher introduced him.

"Please welcome Griffin Silk," she said. "It's Griffin's first day and I want you all to make him feel welcome."

And later on, when he had correctly answered some of her questions, he heard loudly whispered comments about him being "teacher's pet," so he decided not to answer any more.

At lunchtime it was even worse.

"So, is it *Mister* Griffin?" asked one of the boys, with his face uncomfortably close to Griffin's.

"No, just Griffin. Daddy named me after the mythical beast."

"Oh, the mythical beast!"

The boy who had spoken first doubled over with laughter, holding his sides as though they hurt, and the others joined in.

When they tired of laughing at the explanation of Griffin's name, they pulled at the stiff new cloth of the gray school shorts and pale blue shirt that Nell had bought him. They stood on his elastic-sided boots, the gritty soles of their dirty sneakers grinding into the shiny leather.

He felt someone tug his long hair. "Why don't ya get a haircut, ya girl?"

"Leave it, you might catch nits off him," said the tallest boy, the one they called Scotty. Griffin stared into his lunch box and wished they would go away. But he felt the wooden slatted bench bow beneath him, and from the corner of his eye he saw Scotty sit down close by.

"So, Mister Griffin, I've heard there's a whole tribe of you Silks live up on the hill. How come none of the others come to school here?"

"We all learned at home from Mama, till she got sick. My sisters go to the upper school on the bus now," Griffin explained. His eyes were fixed on the unopened sandwiches that Nell had made for him.

"How many sisters ya got?"

"There's Scarlet and Indigo and Violet and Amber and Saffron and—"

"Geez, what sorta names are they? Did ya daddy name them all after some imaginary critters too?" The other boys laughed at Scotty's cleverness.

"Oh no, Daddy calls them his Rainbow Girls. You see, my grandma Nell's favorite color is scarlet and Mama's favorite flowers are violets and—"

"So, you're the baby, huh?" interrupted Scotty rudely. "Little Mister Griffin, the bubby beast."

"No!" Griffin had had enough. Recklessly, he slammed the lid of his lunch box shut and stood up. He looked at Scotty and his band of supporters. They stood on a forest of battered legs with scabby knees and filthy, unlaced sneakers, arms folded, waiting edgily for a sign, a word from their leader.

"I'm not a baby. My name is Griffin Silk and I live with my daddy and Nell and my five big sisters, and soon Mama will come home and bring my little sister." Griffin shouted the information in one

long breath. It wasn't really a lie. He'd imagined it in his head so many times that he almost believed it himself.

Scotty and his pals stared openmouthed as Griffin turned his back and walked away from them. His heart thumped in his chest, his cheeks burned, and his legs shook, but Griffin kept walking toward the cool, welcoming shade under the outstretched limbs of the elms near the playground.

Behind him he heard Scott McAllister's voice, but it seemed less frightening now.

"Geez, didn't I say there was a tribe of 'em? An' there's another one too! Another girl. No wonder he's a crybaby, with all them women in the family," he told his friends, pretending not to notice their admiration for the way Griffin had stood up to him. Then he called out after Griffin's retreating figure. "Hey, kid, your old folks would've been runnin' outta names for the last brat, wouldn't they? Whatcha call the little one then? Eh?"

Griffin didn't reply right away. He wasn't being rude. It was just the way of things in the Silk household.

Daddy was a big fan of cogitation. Sometimes it took him three days to work out his best response. He said it was fine to cogitate if you didn't know something straight off, that you got much better answers if you thought a bit before you spoke.

Griffin reached the comfort of the shade and sat down on the grass. He pulled off his stiff new boots and socks. He sniffed his socks and then tucked them into his boots. He opened his lunch box and unwrapped his sandwich.

He lifted up the top piece of bread to see what was inside—honey and peanut butter—and then closed it. He took a bite and lay back on the grass in the dappled shade. The elm leaves jostled against one another in the lazy spring breeze, rustling like a lady's taffeta dress.

"Tishkin," he said quietly, and it was the first time he had said the name aloud, although he had heard it inside his head for a long, long time. "Tishkin, that's what I call her." And he smiled at the sound of it as the elm leaves repeated after him, "Tishkin, Tishkin."

Princess Layla

At the end of the day, Scotty McAllister and his gang left their lockers, trailing school-bags, shoelaces, and laughter behind them into the bright afternoon light.

Griffin watched from the step outside the faded green door of Saint Benedict's Primary School. They rode their bikes down the powdery footpath, skidding their wheels and sending up clouds of cocoa-colored dust. Griffin dawdled down the path, hoping they wouldn't turn and see him, but they were long gone by the time he reached the front gate.

The road that led to Griffin's house was little used, except by the Silk family. No one remembered if it had a real name or not. Everyone at Cameron's Creek called it the Silk Road. It meandered between the paddocks, a generous ribbon of gravel with a mean smear of tar up the middle and dribbling off the edges. Clumps of blowfly grass and scaly gray lichens trespassed undisturbed on the road's ragged borders. Rusty-headed rushes grew in the boggy ditches on either side of the road and made a pleasant home for frogs and other moisture-loving creatures. The Silk Road, where Griffin lived, was in Australia, but he'd once read a book about China and was surprised to learn there was a Silk Road there as well.

Griffin sat down in the shade of the feathery blue leaves of a cootamundra wattle. He dangled his socks and his hot, aching feet in the thin stream of water in the ditch. He wriggled his toes, teasing the tiny black tadpoles that swam in the clear ripples. If only he could go barefoot to school like he did at home, but then the kids would laugh at him even more, he supposed.

He wished that he could tell Nell about the clothes she had bought him, without hurting her feelings. None of the other kids wore these kinds of clothes. Maybe Daddy and Nell wouldn't send him back to school, once they found out what it was like.

He cheered up a little at that thought, fished his socks from the water, and carefully turned them inside out in case any tadpoles had swum inside. He wrung the water from them, tied them together at the toe ends, and tucked them inside his shirt collar to cool his neck. He remembered the remains of his lunchtime sandwich and took it out of his schoolbag to eat.

Griffin's heart jolted when he heard someone call out, "Hey, wait up!" He shrank farther back under the canopy of the tree, hoping whoever it was would pass by. He didn't want any more trouble today.

"I can still see you." The persistent voice came closer.

Griffin peered out from his hiding place and saw it was a girl. She was whip-thin, smaller than he was. She knelt down when she reached the tree and looked under its fringe at Griffin.

"Hello," she said. "I've been trying to catch up with you. My name's Layla." She smiled at him, and though she had more gaps than teeth, her whole face seemed to smile. Her eyes were the color of forget-me-nots, and her long, straight hair was as shiny as a crow's wing.

But it wasn't Layla's smile or her cheerful greeting or her blue, blue eyes or even her shiny black hair that made Griffin come out from under the tree. It was the daisy chain that she wore like a crown on her head.

When Griffin was very small, Mama and the girls used to push him up the hills in the old wicker baby carriage. In springtime, when the yellow cape-weed bloomed and covered the hills like custard over steamed puddings, they would make daisy chains all afternoon. They made crowns for themselves and for Griffin, and when they put them on, they would magically become queens or princesses and Griffin would always be the king or a prince. Sometimes they would try to make chains long enough to reach all the way from the top of the hill to home again.

By the February when Tishkin was born, Griffin's fingers had grown nimble enough to carefully splice the sappy stems, to make the slits just big enough to thread the next flower stem through.

How well he remembered when he and Blue the dog had been allowed to go to the hills by themselves.

It was on that afternoon that he had gathered the first few daisies of the season and made a coronet, baby-size, just perfect for Tishkin. He took it home and put it on the lid of his toy box. He knew that the flowers would close their petals and go to sleep when he did but that when the sun streamed through the window in the morning, they would open, like yellow eyelashes around dark eyes.

But when Griffin woke up the next morning, he found that Mama and Tishkin had gone away, so he hid the crown of daisies in a special place.

It was still there.

So Griffin knew all about daisy chains. He understood right away that a person who believed in the magic of daisies, a person skilled in the art of crown making, was likely to be an uncommon kind of person.

That was why he came out from his hiding place to talk to Layla.

"I'm pleased to meet you, Princess Layla," he said gravely, offering his hand to the princess. "I'm Griffin Silk."

The princess answered, "I know. I heard you telling Scotty McAllister. That's why I came. I want you to tell me about the beast. You know, the magical beast that your daddy—"

"Mythical beast," Griffin corrected her. "It's a sort of imaginary creature that people told stories about."

"You mean like a bunyip or the abominable snowman?"

"Sort of. The griffin had the head and wings of an eagle and the body of a lion. If you came to my

house, Daddy would tell you all about it. He's got pictures of it in a book."

Princess Layla's forget-me-not eyes looked down at her feet. She kicked at the loose gravel with her pink sneaker, and her crown slipped a little till it was crooked on her forehead.

"I don't know. I'll have to ask my mother first," she said, because even princesses have to ask their mothers some things. Then she looked up and brightened. "I'll ask her tonight and tell you at school tomorrow."

The thought of another day at school flicked darkly across Griffin's mind, but it might not be so bad if Princess Layla was there.

"Okay," he said. "Do you want some tadpoles?"

Empty Places

Blue was red with white freckles, or white with red freckles, depending on which way you looked at him. He was born under the fruit tree outside Griffin's bedroom window on the sixteenth day of the third spring of Griffin's life.

The tree was in blossom and the blackbirds sang on the morning Blue was born. It was clear from the beginning that he was an uncommon sort of dog. His head was too big and his legs were too short and he couldn't hear the blackbirds singing.

And long after his brothers and sisters had gone to good homes, nobody seemed to want Blue, except Griffin. And that was very good, thought Griffin, because Blue was exactly the sort of dog that he wanted.

Blue waited all day by the corner post in the front paddock for Griffin's return. Nell understood the power of love and didn't try to persuade him to come back to the house. Instead, she carried a bucket of water down the hill and put it in the shade for him. Blue lowered his ears in recognition of her kindness but didn't take his eyes from the road.

Though Blue couldn't hear, he had other gifts, which were especially powerful. He could feel the vibrations that people's footsteps made on the earth, even over distances as great as that between the corner post and Joe Canning's dam. He could even tell which member of the Silk family made them. And though Griffin's boots were in his schoolbag on that hot afternoon, and his bare feet made very little sound, Blue's tail began to thump on the ground with joy, before he could even see the top of Griffin's head rising up over the crest of the hill.

Griffin wrapped his arms around Blue's neck and smelled the sunshine on his thick, dappled coat and the sweet, dry earth on the pads of his feet. They lay there for a while, content in each other's company, then walked together up the long red gravel driveway to the house. Blue stretched out on the porch and went to sleep, exhausted by his long day of waiting.

The screen door slammed behind Griffin. The striped canvas blinds were pulled down all around the porch to keep the house cool, and he blinked at the soft daytime dusk inside. His dusty feet left a ghostly trail behind him on the bare floor of the hallway. The house was full of quietness, as though his ears were stuffed with cotton wool.

Griffin stopped to listen to the small sounds of the afternoon that mostly got lost among the busy living noises of his large family. It was so quiet that he could almost hear his heart beating. He unbuttoned his shirt and put his hand on his chest, over his heart. He remembered when Mama had let him press his face against her big, soft belly, to feel the beginnings of Tishkin. It seemed so long ago, so much longer than a year and a half.

He walked into Daddy's room and looked at the bed where Tishkin had been born. In the corner of the room was Tishkin's crib. Mama had painted it blue and yellow, the colors of summer. He dropped his schoolbag on the floor, climbed up onto the bed, and wriggled into the saggy bit in the middle. He shut his eyes and tried to remember the smell of Mama. He turned his back to the empty crib.

Empty Places

He was still asleep when the school bus let the girls off at the bottom of the driveway. Their noisy chatter and the crunch of the gravel under their hard black school shoes drew Griffin out of his dreams, like a bubble floating upward from the silent darkness of the ocean toward the glittering, sunlit surface above. The bubble burst and he opened his eyes and stretched, and his world changed from misty grays to sharp color, restful silence to sound.

He went, pink-cheeked from sleep and unnoticed, into the kitchen and sat at Mama's place at the table. The girls were trying to tell Nell about their day, all at the same time, like a flock of parrots.

Nell turned around from where she had been peeling potatoes in the sink and looked right at Griffin, as though she had known all along that he was there behind her. She dried her hands on her

apron as she came to him and cupped his chin in her warm palm. She studied his face over the top of her spectacles.

"Tough day?" she asked, and Griffin knew she had seen him sleeping. He nodded.

The girls had more questions, questions that he didn't particularly want to answer, so he said, "I met a princess on the way home."

"Princess who?" asked Scarlet.

"Princess Layla."

"How did you know she was a princess?" asked Indigo.

"Well, she would have told him, wouldn't she?" said Violet. "Did she, Griff? Did she tell you?"

"She said her name was Layla, but she didn't have to tell me she was a princess. I knew as soon as I saw the crown."

"What sort of crown?" Amber wanted to know.

"You know, a daisy-chain crown, of course!"

said Griffin. "They were only skinny little daisies, but she'd made a lovely crown and her hair was as black as Zeus's feathers." Zeus was perched on the windowsill above the sink waiting for an opportunity to steal some of the dinner Nell was preparing. He squawked in recognition of his name and leaped down on to the sink.

"Get off there this minute, you wicked creature," said Nell sternly, but she didn't seem to mind when he hopped onto her shoulder.

"Maybe she was Zeus in disguise," said Saffron, holding out her arm for Zeus to stand on.

"Who was?" asked Violet.

"The princess," answered Saffron. Despite being eleven and the youngest of the Rainbow Girls, she, like Griffin, was a grade ahead of other children her age and went to the upper school along with her sisters. Saffron knew almost everything there was to know about mythology. "The ancient Greeks believed that Zeus was the ruler of heaven and could transform himself into all kinds of different things, like swans and showers of gold. Maybe our Zeus is really the ruler of heaven and he changed himself into a crow and then into the Princess Layla."

"No, it wasn't Zeus," Griffin said firmly. "I saw her at school and she was just a girl then. She didn't change into a princess until she put her crown on. Anyway, she's coming to our house tomorrow and then you'll be able to see that she's not Zeus." But he thought he might take Zeus to school, just to make sure.

He didn't notice what the girls said next, because he heard his father's truck and ran outside. He saw the old pickup stop at the bottom of the hill. His father got out to open the gate, then climbed back into the cabin. Griffin waved, and the horn sounded as the truck moved slowly through the open gateway. The sun blazed low on the horizon, and Griffin shaded his eyes with his hand, trying to see if there was anyone sitting in the passenger seat. But the sunset glared back at him from the windshield.

The battered truck crept slowly up the hill, and Griffin's hopeful heart grew heavy when he realized that Daddy was alone again. Every day for the last four months or so he'd done the same, tried to pretend that he wasn't looking for Mama. When all the time he secretly imagined her sitting there next to Daddy, with a big smile on her face, and Tishkin would be there in the truck with them. But today, just like all the other days, there was only Daddy in the truck.

Griffin waited until the truck stopped and his father jumped down from the cabin and swept him up in his arms.

"Fly away, my little one, my golden Griffin," he

said, and began to spin like a carousel with his strong, warm hands under Griffin's armpits supporting him, lifting him. Around and around he turned, slowly at first. Then, as they gained momentum, Griffin stretched out his arms like the wings of an eagle and lifted his face to the sun. It touched his eyes like fire, and he closed them and soared away, to find Mama in that beautiful place where nobody ever had bad thoughts, and everyone loved her and brought her cups of tea and posies of violets whenever she felt like them, and there was nothing at all to make her sad.

Maybe Mama was so happy that she didn't want to come home. Or maybe she wasn't coming home because she knew about the thoughts in Griffin's head. He hoped no one knew about them, but Mama sometimes knew things that no one told her. As his heart grew sadder, his wings became heavy and he felt himself falling from the sky.

Slowly they stopped spinning, and Griffin folded his wings around his father's chest.

"Not today, Griff, not today," said Daddy, and buried his face in Griffin's soft yellow hair. Griffin felt his father's warm breath when he whispered, "Have courage, my lionheart."

Griffin wondered how it was that small boys and mothers and fathers could sometimes read the feelings in each other's hearts, even when the words that came out didn't match them, and sometimes without a word being spoken at all. He knew in that moment how much Daddy missed Mama and Tishkin too, and he put his arms around his father's neck to comfort him. He wondered if Daddy would love him quite so much if he knew whose fault it was that Mama and Tishkin had gone away.

A Bird in the Bag

Tuesday started off badly. First there was the matter of the missing lunch box. Nell had made Griffin's sandwich and wrapped it in waxy paper, but the lunch box was nowhere to be found. Neither was Griffin.

Scarlet found him, lying on his stomach in the garden watching the skinks dart in and out from the foxgloves.

"Shhhh," he whispered when she called him. "I'm trying to catch Zeus a snack for recess."

"Recess? What are you talking about?"

He realized he'd made a mistake. Scarlet would tell Nell if she found out about his plan to take Zeus to school.

"Oh, nothing. I just thought Zeus might like a snack and I'm trying to catch a little lizard for him. So go away, you're scaring them."

"Good job. You're a disgusting little grub, Griffin William Silk."

"Am not. Crows eat lizards in the wild."

"Are so. Zeus doesn't need lizards. He gets plenty of other food." As Griffin stood up, Scarlet pointed accusingly at the smears of soil on the front of his shirt. "Look at your good school shirt. Nell's going to be really mad at you now. She can't find your lunch box. Where is it?"

"I caught some tadpoles in it for Princess Layla," he said, trying to brush the marks from his shirt before he went inside. "She'll bring it back today."

Griffin was pleased when Scarlet stopped trying to organize him and had walked down the driveway to catch the bus. He waited until he heard the bus driving away, then he went to the clothesline, where his grandmother was hanging out the towels.

"Lift me up, Nell," he coaxed, and she boosted him up until he could grip the sturdy metal crossbar on the rotary clothesline.

"Oooh!" she groaned. "You're getting too heavy to lift."

"Push me please, Nell!" She put a hand on each side of his waist and pulled him around until the clothesline began to revolve.

"Faster, Nell, faster!" he said.

Nell stopped, out of breath. "Oh, I'm getting too old for this sort of thing!" She laughed, puffing.

She stood and watched as the clothesline slowly came to a stop, and then caught Griffin in her arms.

"You'd better start walking or you'll be late for school," she said, but she didn't put him down right away. "It won't always be this bad, you'll see."

He kissed Nell goodbye and promised her he wouldn't forget to ask Layla for his lunch box, then he walked back to the house.

Griffin slept at the back of the house, where the porch had been filled in with weatherboards and glass louvers to make more room as the Silk family expanded. He went into his room and picked up his schoolbag, then collected his lunch from the kitchen. He patted Blue, who was in his favorite spot on the front porch, and then called softly for Zeus.

Zeus didn't come. Griffin stepped down from the porch and called again. He couldn't call too loudly or Nell might hear and come to investigate. He walked around to the side of the house where the henhouse was, and there was Zeus, pecking at the vegetable scraps that Indigo had saved from last night's dinner.

"Zeus," he called. Zeus looked up, cocked his head to one side, and stared at Griffin with his one white eye. "Come on, Zeus," he called softly. But Zeus was hungry, and even vegetable scraps were better than nothing. He returned to his meal.

Griffin opened his bag and unwrapped his sandwich. He took out half and put the rest back in his bag. He opened the gate of the hens' yard and went in. He squatted down in the straw and held out the piece of sandwich. Zeus was tempted. He came closer to see what the boy was offering, and Griffin slowly drew his hand in closer to the opening of his bag. He let Zeus have a taste of the sandwich. It had sardines inside. Zeus liked sardines. The crow took another peck and another, not realizing that all the time Griffin was luring him closer and closer to the bag. Griffin threw the crusts into the bottom of his bag and held the opening wide. Zeus lunged at the food again, and suddenly he was in complete darkness. Griffin had quickly zipped the bag shut, and Zeus was trapped. He squawked angrily.

"Shh, Zeus. It's all right. I'll let you out when I get down the road a bit." He slung the bag onto his shoulders and hurried down the driveway. Blue trotted along behind him, with his nose in the air. He couldn't hear the sounds coming from Griffin's bag, but he could smell what was left of the sardine sandwich.

Griffin looked behind him to make sure Nell hadn't heard all the noise. He was almost to the gate at the bottom of the driveway before she appeared around the side of the house. Griffin turned and waved to her. He was too far away for Nell to see that his schoolbag appeared to have a life of its own, and though she could hear Zeus's angry protests, she couldn't tell where they were coming from.

Griffin did let Zeus out, but not until they were out of sight of the house. Zeus was most indignant and wouldn't sit on Griffin's shoulder until he had been given the other half of the sardine sandwich. It had been trampled flat in the bottom of the bag anyway, so Griffin decided it wasn't much use keeping it for his lunch.

Bringing a crow to school is no simple matter. It took a great deal more time for Griffin to get there than it would have had he left Zeus at home. Just as he passed the wattle tree where he had met Princess Layla the day before, he heard the school bell ring. He began to run. Zeus clung to his shoulder, tearing little holes in the cloth of the shirt where his sharp claws dug in. But Griffin couldn't stop. It was only his second day at school and he was going to be late!

A Fearless Friend

The last of the children were disappearing around the corner of the classroom as Griffin ran down the corridor, without leaving his bag in his locker. The teacher was writing on the blackboard and had her back to the class. Griffin edged around the doorway and slid behind his desk, hoping his lateness would go unnoticed.

In his haste, he had forgotten Zeus clinging to his shoulder. But it took only moments for the other children to see the crow. Miss Beaumont heard the excited whispering and then the giggling and was so annoyed by it that she turned around before she had put the period at the end of the sentence she had written.

Miss Beaumont blinked, quite a lot, when she first noticed Zeus. The classroom became very quiet. For a moment not a word was spoken and, it seemed, not even a breath taken, while the students waited till their teacher stopped blinking and began to speak. Her voice quavered like a gate swinging on a rusty hinge.

"I see you have a crow on your shoulder, Griffin Silk."

Zeus stopped preening his feathers and cocked his head to listen.

"Yes, miss. His name is Zeus."

Zeus acknowledged his name with a pleased little squawk that sounded like a fingernail scraping the blackboard.

Miss Beaumont winced. "And where did you get him from?"

"Nell found him near the Brussels sprouts when he was just hatched. He didn't have any feathers and he's blind in one eye. Nell thinks he must have fallen out of a nest and she looked after him till . . ."

Griffin heard the whispers and laughter behind him and recognized the voice of the boy called Scotty when he hissed behind his hand, "Told ya so. They're all weird, and the old lady's a witch."

"Silence, Scott McAllister," warned Miss Beaumont sternly. "Griffin," she said, "don't you think it would be better if . . . Zeus was free?"

"Oh, he is free, miss," Griffin assured the teacher. "He goes wherever and whenever he wants to. He comes inside at mealtimes and sleeps on the end of Nell's bed and . . ." Griffin stopped. He could barely make himself heard above the noise in the classroom. Zeus was getting nervous. His claws were digging into Griffin's shoulder, which was already scratched and sore. Suddenly Zeus flapped his wings and flew up to sit above the window.

"Class, that will be enough noise," shouted Miss Beaumont, banging on her desk with a ruler.

"Now, Griffin, I'm afraid we can't have a wild creature loose in the classroom," she went on. "If you let him go outside, will he fly away?"

"I don't know, miss," said Griffin miserably, wondering why he had ever thought that it would be a good idea to bring Zeus to school.

"Can you get him to come down from there?"

"Yes, miss."

"I want you to take him to the janitor's closet down by the staff room and lock him in there. Nobody but the cleaner uses that room. The crow will be quite safe in there until you go home."

Griffin raised his forearm and called to Zeus. If he hadn't felt so sorry that Zeus was going to be locked in a closet all day, Griffin would have been quite pleased by the other children's gasps of admiration at Zeus's gliding flight and perfect landing on his master's outstretched arm.

Griffin began the long walk down the corridor, tempted to keep on walking and go home. He stopped at the door to the janitor's closet and wished that Zeus really was the ruler of heaven. Then he could send down a great jagged bolt of lightning to hit the school, or change himself into something big enough to frighten Scotty McAllister.

But Zeus stayed just as he was, a friendly, shiny black crow with one white eye.

"I'm sorry, Zeus," said Griffin. Zeus cocked his head and listened and then nuzzled Griffin's cheek with his smooth black beak. Griffin opened the door and turned on the light inside the little room. There was a stainless steel trough in the corner.

Griffin turned on the tap and filled it halfway with water. "There's some water for you to drink," he said as he felt around in the bottom of his bag, which he still hadn't taken to his locker. He found an apple and put it down beside the sink. "You can have this to keep you going till we get home. I'll leave the light on for you," he said, as Zeus hopped down to taste the apple. Griffin backed out into the corridor and closed the door.

It seemed that everyone at school, even in Layla's grade, had heard about the incident in Miss Beaumont's classroom, including the rumor about Nell being a witch.

"Did ya ride yer grandma's broomstick to school today, Mr. Griffin?" someone from Scotty McAllister's gang called out at first recess. Layla climbed on top of the monkey bars. Griffin was

afraid a sudden gust of wind might blow her away, but what she lacked in size, she made up for in courage. She was fearless.

She stood up, her pink-sneakered feet clinging to the worn metal rungs, and with her hands planted firmly on her hips, she shouted above their taunts, "If my grandmother was a witch . . ." She paused then, waiting for the mob's attention. "I said, if *my* grandmother was a witch, the first thing I would ask her to do would be to put a spell on all of you. And the second thing would be to send her pet crow after you, to peck your eyes out! So if I was you guys, I wouldn't be saying too much to my friend Griffin."

She stood there on top of the monkey bars, balancing precariously on the narrow rungs. Her eyes blazed ferociously and dared anyone to defy her. Griffin's thoughts flicked to the janitor's closet. He wondered if Zeus was still there, or . . .

"*Is* your grandmother a witch?" asked Layla after Scotty and his pals had wandered away, still throwing insults over their shoulders.

"I don't think so," said Griffin. "I never asked her."

"Oh." Layla sounded disappointed. "Scotty McAllister told my brother, Patrick, that she was."

"Did you ask your mother if you could come to my house?"

"Yes, she said yes. Does she have a cat?" Layla was still investigating the possibility of having a friend whose grandmother was a witch.

"No, she says they eat the blue wrens and silvereyes." But, he thought sadly, she does have a pet crow, one that's locked in the janitor's closet. He decided not to mention that Saffron thought Princess Layla was an incarnation of Zeus. "Nell said you could stay for dinner."

"Do you think she'll make a brew for dinner?"

"I don't know if she's got a recipe for brew. I'll ask her. Will you stay for dinner if she makes a brew?"

"I'll have to phone my mother. Do you have a phone?"

"Yes."

"Good." Griffin was pleased to stop talking about witches and brews. They shared Layla's snack, and he began to feel better.

"Did you bring your crown today?" he asked.

"No, it's dead. But I know where there are more daisies. We can get some on the way home. We can make a necklace for Zeus too!"

The Kingdom of Silk

Nell was sitting on the red vinyl couch on the porch when Griffin, Layla, and Zeus arrived. The sun had wilted the crowns they had made on the way home, but Nell still recognized royalty when she saw it and was quick to stand in their presence.

"Good afternoon, Your Highnesses," she said with a graceful curtsy, "may I introduce myself?" Griffin nodded while Layla stood speechless with surprise at Nell's appearance. She wore green rubber dishwashing gloves right up to her elbows, with red fingernails painted on the ends and lots of sparkling bead bracelets over the tops of them. On her head was a magnificent silver plastic tiara decorated with glass rubies, which she had borrowed from Violet for the occasion. Her long black skirt trailed behind her, showing only the toes of her elastic-sided boots.

"I am Nell, your fairy grandmother," she said, rummaging around in a deep pocket in the side of her skirt. She took out a long, slender, silver-frosted stick with a glittering star attached to one end and tapped each of them lightly on the shoulder with it.

Then she addressed the crow. "How splendid you look in your yellow ruffle, Lord Zeus. It flatters your dusky complexion." Zeus flapped over to sit on her arm, the daisy chain swinging around his glossy neck as he flew. "I trust Lord Zeus behaved himself in a comely manner at school," said Nell in her most fairy-grandmotherly voice, and Griffin knew that he was forgiven for taking the bird.

"I don't think he liked it much," said Griffin. "I think he'd rather have stayed at home with you."

"I have prepared some refreshments for Your Majesties, if you would care to follow me down to the Cox's orange pippin," said Nell.

Layla giggled and whispered to Griffin as they followed Nell around the side of the house toward the dam. "Whatever is the Cox's orange pippin?"

Griffin opened his eyes wide with surprise. "Oh, that's the name of our apple tree. You see, everything in the Kingdom of Silk has a name."

Layla giggled again and said, "We should have made a daisy chain for . . . your grandmother. What should I call her, Griffin?"

"Um, Fairy Grandmother would be nice, I think," said Griffin.

Nell had come to a stop beneath a medium-size

spreading tree. Its gnarled old branches were mottled with yellow and gray lichen and bowed low by a burden of blossom. Beneath its branches was a small table covered with a white cloth, as lacy as a cobweb. Beside the table, in the shaggy green grass, were two large, plump purple cushions dimpled in their middles with buttons as round and yellow as full moons.

"Would you care to be seated, Your Majesties?" asked the fairy grandmother.

Griffin and Layla sat down on the cushions.

"Can I take my boots off now?" asked Griffin.

"Your Majesty may dispose of his boots whenever he wishes," answered the fairy grandmother. And she filled two tumblers with crushed ice that sparkled like diamonds and liquid the color of honey from a glass pitcher on the table.

Griffin took his boots off, and Layla removed

her pink sneakers and frilly socks. Griffin noticed her toenails were painted blue with little red hearts and sparkles on them. Just like a real princess would have, he thought.

Nell put the drinks on a tray along with a plate of bread and butter covered with sprinkles. "Would you care for a glass of hummingbird nectar or a triangle of fairy bread, Your Majesties?" she asked, passing the tray first to Layla and then to Griffin.

"Thank you, Fairy Grandmother," said Layla, helping herself to some of each.

"You're welcome, Princess Layla." Nell set the tray back on the table after Griffin had taken something to eat and drink. She whispered some magic words and blew a handful of apple blossoms into the air. Then she made her way back to the house, taking Zeus with her.

"Oh, Griffin, you're so lucky to live here and to

have such a lovely grandma," said Layla after they
had eaten their way through a small mountain of
fairy-bread triangles.

Fred and Ginger, Amber's two geese, strolled by,
took the crusts from Griffin's outstretched hand in
their carrot-colored beaks, then sailed serenely out
into the middle of the pond. The children lay
sprawled on the cushions, looking up at the scraps

of blue sky between the leaves and blossoms of the Cox's orange pippin.

"I think I can see a face looking down at me," said Layla dreamily.

Griffin sat up quickly. "Where? Show me." He came and lay down next to Layla and she pointed.

"Up there, see? Oh no, I think it's changing. I don't know if it is a face after all, maybe it's a—"

"What sort of face was it?" Griffin interrupted. "Was it a grownup's face or a baby's?"

"Oh, I don't know, just a face." Layla sat up. "Why, why is it so important?"

"Nothing," said Griffin, and his ears burned. "I'm sorry, it was nothing." But he wondered if Layla had seen the same face that he sometimes saw. If someone else saw it too, that would mean he wasn't just imagining it, wouldn't it?

The Ñaming Day Books

When the sun went down, the daisies shut their bright eyes. Prince Griffin and Princess Layla took off their crowns and became normal children again. The fairy grandmother also disappeared.

Layla telephoned her mother and stayed for dinner, and although Nell hadn't cooked up a brew, the meal was delicious. Layla decided that even if Nell wasn't a witch or a fairy grandmother, there was still something very magical about her.

Daddy was late coming home, so Nell said Griffin and Layla could go up into the front room, which was only used on special occasions. They could look at the Naming Day Books while she and the Rainbow Girls washed the dishes.

Griffin opened the door of the sideboard with a little golden key and took out six large, heavy books, one by one. Then he and Layla lay down on the pink cabbage roses on the worn-out carpet square in the middle of the room with the Naming Day Books in front of them.

The first book was Scarlet's. The cover was made of wood and finely carved with beautiful scrolled patterns. In the middle of the cover the name Scarlet was inlaid in a lighter colored wood and beneath it, the date of Scarlet's birthday.

"Can I touch it?" asked Layla.

"Oh yes, it's best if you feel it," said Griffin.

"Daddy says you can't know something properly by just looking."

Their fingers explored all the nooks and crannies and the gullies and ridges of the landscape engraved on Scarlet's Naming Day Book.

"Daddy carved the covers for all the books," said Griffin, "and each one is different. Mama made the paper for the pages inside."

They opened Scarlet's book. The first page was covered with tissue, and the paper beneath was almost transparent, flecked with flower petals, leaves, and tiny seeds. In the center of the page was a lock of corn-gold hair, curled like a comma and tied with scarlet embroidery silk. On the second page was a poem, written in red ink in perfect, even handwriting with long, curly tails on the letters.

"Can you read it?" asked Layla.

"I know it by heart," said Griffin. "It's called 'For Scarlet.'

Now that you are, there is color in my life,
But should we part you will remain even then,
For Scarlet is my heart, my lips, the blood that gives
    me life.

Mama wrote it for Scarlet's Naming Day Ceremony."

"But what does it mean?"

"I think it means that even when they're not together, Mama feels like Scarlet is with her."

"It's a very nice poem."

They turned over the pages, one by one, and looked at the photographs of the celebration that took place on the day Scarlet received her name. Griffin explained how his father liked to wait until one whole year after the birth of the baby before

holding the Naming Day, so that they had time to get to know the baby and to choose a name to suit. Layla thought that was a very good idea.

"Can we look at your book now?" she asked after they had closed Scarlet's. Griffin liked to look at his own book best of all. He remembered when he was much younger, sitting in this very same place with his big sisters, who were also much smaller then. They had turned the pages and pointed to the pictures and the words, over and over, so that by the time he was old enough to look at his book all by himself, he knew every little bit by heart. It was as though he had remembered the ceremony from being there. He crossed his legs and placed his book carefully in his lap.

"Come and sit next to me and I'll tell you all about it," he said to Layla. He explained that the carving on the front of his book represented the griffin. They traced the outlines of the wooden feathers on its proud eagle's head and the strong, outstretched wings. They stroked the rippling muscles of the beast. Inside, written in the same beautiful handwriting as Scarlet's book, was the myth of the griffin. When they came to the photographs, Layla saw that they had been taken outside under the Cox's orange pippin.

"That's where we were today," she said, pointing to a photograph of Griffin's family gathered around a large trestle table down by the dam.

"Yes, all the girls dressed up in Nell's clothes, high heels, and big hats and handbags and long dresses—"

"And lipstick!" Layla pointed out in awe.

Griffin's eyes moved from Layla's face back to the book. He looked at the photograph of the girls dancing and holding their big hats so they wouldn't blow away, and their lipstick smiles were as big as clowns' mouths. Nell was sitting in the long grass with her back to the trunk of the tree, fanning her face with a lace-edged handkerchief. Daddy was holding Griffin right up high and close over his heart. And there was Mama, with her yellow hair streaming, laughing and sprinkling flower petals over him. That was his favorite photograph. He stared and stared at the photo until, from somewhere far away, he heard words fluttering through his head like apple blossom petals floating on the breeze. They were the words Daddy had said when he gave him his name.

"We welcome you to the Silk family and offer you the name of Griffin William Silk. May you rise up on wings as the eagle and may your heart have the courage of the lion." Then Daddy's next words trickled slowly like warm oil into his ear, gentle and soothing. "You are the pot of gold at the end of the rainbow, the period at the end of the Silk family, and the icing on the cake."

But then Tishkin had come. Griffin closed the book.

"Can we look at your baby sister's book now?"

"No."

"Why not?"

Griffin had started putting the books back where they came from. When he had put the last one away, he took the key from his pocket and locked the sideboard. Then he turned around and answered Layla's question.

"Because there isn't one."

"You mean it isn't finished?"

"No, it isn't started."

The Gift of
Reading Hearts

It was a long time before Layla asked Griffin any more about his baby sister, who had gone away, whose crib waited empty next to the big bed where she was born. It wasn't that Layla didn't want to ask. There were often questions inside her head. Sometimes they got as far as the end of her tongue. It was just as well that some of the gaps were filling up with new teeth, and she could close them tightly before it was too late and the thoughts turned into words, because Layla somehow knew that Griffin didn't want to talk about his sister.

Layla came home with Griffin often after school and almost always stayed for dinner. She learned to recognize the sound of the beat-up truck at the bottom of the driveway above the noise of the Rainbow Girls, and sometimes she heard it before Griffin.

Griffin soon realized that Layla had the gift of reading people's hearts just like he and Mama and Daddy, and like Tishkin before she went away. He didn't mind that Layla knew he watched the windshield of Daddy's truck for a glimpse of Mama. He hoped she couldn't see the other things that he didn't want anyone to know, because if she ever did find out, she might not want to be his friend anymore. She might go away too.

Nell had told him that things would get better

at school, and she was right. With a friend like Layla, anything was bearable. Just as the newness wore off his clothes and boots, the newness wore off Griffin Silk, and that seemed to make him less interesting to the other children at school. Not to Layla, but to people like Scotty McAllister and his gang. But then something happened to Griffin that made him blend in more than ever, and that was the doing of Layla Elliott.

It happened when Griffin was invited to play at Layla's house one afternoon after school. Mrs. Elliott had never been the sort of person who liked to play dress-up, and she had long ago forgotten the pleasure of make-believe. She gave Layla and Griffin a glass of cold lemonade each and a packet of potato chips to share and told them to amuse themselves while she prepared dinner. So they went to Layla's room.

There were still lots of things that Griffin didn't

know about Layla. He found out one of them that afternoon. Layla wanted to be a hairdresser when she was old enough. She practiced on her family whenever they would allow it. But her father had very little hair left, and her mother was almost always busy, and her brother, Patrick, said that it was a sissy thing to do. Even when she was given the opportunity, she was allowed only to wash and dry, comb and curl, never to cut or dye. She had practiced cutting and dyeing on her dolls' hair, but the trouble with that was that it never grew back again and black marker wasn't very good for dyeing dolls' hair.

It was hot on the afternoon that Griffin came to play, and Layla tied her own hair up high in a ponytail.

"That's better," she said, swishing the hair from side to side. "It's much cooler this way." She looked longingly at Griffin's hair. "Do you want me to tie yours back in a little piggy tail, Griff?" she coaxed.

"If you want to," he answered, barely looking up from the comic book he had found in her room. He was used to his sisters doing all manner of things to his hair.

Layla combed Griffin's hair while he read. He found it very restful, reading and having his hair combed.

After a while, Layla said, "Maybe I could snip just a tiny bit off the front, so it won't get in your eyes while you're reading."

He peered up through his wispy bangs. "All right, but not too much," he agreed, and went back to his reading.

Layla went out to the kitchen to find some scissors. Griffin was so engrossed in the comic that he didn't even realize she was back, until a chunk of his bangs fell onto the comic. Nell had a saying that she might as well talk to a brick wall as talk to

Griffin when he had a book in his hand. So it escaped his notice that the chunk of hair was rather large. He brushed it to the floor and continued with his reading. Layla, on the other hand, had noticed the large gap left in Griffin's bangs and began to even it up.

Griffin finished his comic and reached up to where his bangs had been. "It feels short," he said.

Layla stood back and surveyed her work. It *was* short, very short. It made the back look even longer. Griffin saw the look on Layla's face and walked over to the dressing table. He looked in the mirror and tugged at what was left of his bangs.

"Maybe if I just trim the back to match, you won't notice it so much," Layla said uncertainly. Griffin wasn't quite sure what to say, but he was saved from saying anything when Mrs. Elliott came to the bedroom door.

"Children," she called, and then she noticed

Layla standing miserably by the dressing table with the scissors in her hand.

"What have you done!" she cried. She clutched Griffin by the shoulders and turned him around to face her. Her face paled, and Griffin thought she was about to faint. Then she began to shriek, "Anthony! Anthony!"

Mr. Elliott came rushing to the door. He summed up the scene in front of him, then put his arm around Mrs. Elliott's shoulders and led her away toward the kitchen. "Now, now, dear, don't worry. I'll look after everything," he told her. As he walked down the hallway, he turned around, and Griffin could have sworn that he winked.

What could have been quite a nasty experience turned out rather well in the end. Mr. Elliott took Griffin and Layla to the barbershop.

"Looks like he needs a number two to sort that out, Tony," said the barber. Twenty minutes later

Griffin came out of the barbershop with a smile on his face and a haircut like the stubble in a cornfield, short and straight and golden.

"All we have to do now is explain this to your grandmother," said Mr. Elliott.

Griffin was pleased that the girls were still swimming in the pond with Ginger and Fred while Mr. Elliott explained to Nell what had happened. Nell ran her hand across the top of Griffin's soft, short hair, then stood back and held up her thumb as though she was looking at a painting in an art gallery. She tilted her head, first this way and then that.

After a few seconds she clicked her tongue against her teeth. "My word, Griffin," she said, "you're as flash as a rat with a gold tooth."

Then Mr. Elliott stopped jingling the loose

coins in his pocket and Layla and Griffin smiled at each other. Nell buttered date scones and made a pot of tea to share with Mr. Elliott.

It was dusk by the time Griffin and Layla went outside to wait for the pickup. The bottom part of the sky was the color of pumpkins, and the top, where the stars were, was the color of Daddy's Bluey jacket. They sat on the porch eating date scones and dangling their bare feet in the marigolds in the garden bed below and listening to the jiminy crickets singing scratchy little love songs to one another.

"How come you're not angry with me, Griff?" Layla asked.

"You're my friend . . . and you didn't mean it. Anyway, now I've got a proper haircut, so Scotty McAllister can't laugh at me anymore."

"How do you know I didn't mean it?"

"Just do. Listen. I can hear Daddy coming!"

The headlights appeared like twin moons, away down at the bottom of the Silk Road.

"Griff, how do you know I didn't mean it?" Layla asked again, and grabbed Griffin's hand.

He turned to look at her and knew that she wouldn't let up until he answered the question. He spoke slowly and carefully. "Daddy says that sometimes, when people know each other really well, they don't need ears to hear and they don't need words to talk. They just know."

"That's what I thought," she said. "It happens to me like that sometimes." She held his hand tighter and whispered. "Griffin . . . your baby sister isn't ever going to come home, is she?"

The Flame of Courage

Griffin Silk closed his eyes. He thought about his namesake, about the great, powerful wings of the eagle. He wanted to spread his wings and fly. High above the Kingdom of Silk he would soar, away from school, away from Scotty McAllister, and away from Layla Elliott, so he wouldn't have to answer her question. He would fly to a safe place, a big, soft nest lined with feathers, to be with his mother. But maybe Mama wouldn't want him there. She might toss him out of the nest, like Zeus's mother had done.

He felt himself falling down, down, and then something warm. He opened his eyes. Layla was beside him, still holding his hand. Inside, he felt something swell like the tiny flare of a match in the darkness. Layla smiled and squeezed his hand and the feeling grew stronger. And though Griffin didn't realize it, the feeling had a name. It was courage.

Griffin had never said the words out loud, because he knew that once they were spoken, it made things real. Once they were said, he couldn't pretend anymore, not to himself, or Layla, or Scotty McAllister, or anyone else. It was hard to move his lips, and his voice seemed to come from a long way away, but the little flame of courage that Layla had lit in his heart grew stronger and he said, "No, Tishkin won't ever come home."

"Tishkin." Layla tasted the name on her tongue,

where it dissolved like fairy floss. "Is that her name?"

"It's what I call her."

"What's her real name?"

"She doesn't have one."

"Why not?"

"Because she went away before we gave her a name."

"Why do you call her Tishkin?"

"Because that's the sound I hear the leaves make, when I see her face looking down at me."

"Oh, so that's who you thought I saw looking down through the Cox's orange pippin?"

"Yes."

"Well, I think it's a beautiful name. Tishkin, Tishkin." Layla repeated the name, and Griffin was pleased that she liked the name he had chosen for his baby sister.

"Why did she go away, Griff?" The flame

burning inside Griffin began to flicker as though someone was trying to blow it out, but he couldn't stop now.

"I think it was because I didn't love her enough."

"Did you tell her that?"

"No, but she must have known." Griffin felt the tears on his cheeks and was glad it was dark so that Layla couldn't see them. The words came quickly as he tried to explain the way things had happened, before his tears put out the last of the flame of courage.

He told Layla how excited everyone had been when Mama had found out she was expecting another baby. Griffin was happy too, in the beginning.

It was such a surprise, because Griffin had been the period at the end of the Silk family. Daddy had said so at his Naming Day Ceremony. He had reminded Daddy about that, and Daddy had

laughed and said that he had made a mistake and Griffin would be a comma instead. Griffin didn't mind that so much, but after Tishkin's arrival came the bad thoughts. Sometimes he wished that she had never been born. It had been nice to have a special place in the family, and now that he was just a comma, no one seemed to have time for him anymore. Everyone was much more interested in the new baby.

"But how could she know that, Griff?" Layla asked. "She was just a baby. How could she read your heart?"

"I don't know, but she must have, because babies are so perfect and not a bit worn out or anything. They don't just die for no reason, do they?"

Layla's blue eyes opened wide. Her chest felt tight, and it was hard to breathe. She hadn't expected this. She'd thought Tishkin was away, somewhere else, maybe with a different family, maybe in a hospital, but somewhere . . . alive. Not this. Not dead. No wonder Griffin hadn't wanted to talk about her.

"Maybe she was sick?" said Layla when she was able to breathe properly again. Her voice sounded like a stranger's to her.

"No, I went to look at her when Mama put her to bed. It was the night before she went away." Griffin remembered looking at his baby sister in the summer-colored crib. She was such a happy little girl. She had a big, round face with red, dimpled cheeks and fuzzy yellow hair like an angel. She smiled at him and blew bubbles, and he put his finger out for her to hold. He remembered thinking how lovely she would look in the daisy coronet he had made for her that afternoon. He kissed her good night, and she laughed and caught his hair in her fat little fingers. Maybe it wasn't so bad having a baby sister after all, he had thought. But it was too late. The next morning he had woken to find the crib empty and Mama and Daddy and Tishkin gone.

"Nell told us that Mama had woken up to feed Tishkin and found that she had died in the night. They took her to the hospital, but the doctors couldn't make her better. And now she's gone because of me and I don't know if Mama will ever come home either."

"Where is your mama?"

"In a kind of hospital."

"Is she sick?"

"Sort of. She misses Tishkin and cries a lot and she can't come home till she's better."

They sat for a while in the darkness. Layla still kept hold of Griffin's hand, and he didn't mind at all. It meant that even though she knew about the horrible thoughts he had had, she still wanted to be his friend.

"Griff," she asked, "why don't you write to your mother and ask her to come home? Maybe she thinks you don't care that she's not at home with you."

"I draw pictures and send them to her sometimes. So do the girls and they write to her."

"Yes, but does anyone tell her that they want her to come home?"

"I don't know."

"Why don't you send her an invitation?"

"An invitation to what?" Suddenly Griffin realized Daddy's truck was at the gate.

"To a party or something. Oh, Griff, I've just had a great idea . . ."

Griffin turned to Layla just as the lights of the truck swept up the drive. Her eyes sparkled.

"Why don't we have a Naming Day Ceremony . . . for Tishkin!"

Homecoming

When a child is born on that most uncommon day, the twenty-ninth of February, arrangements must be made to celebrate the birth at some other time. For leap years occur only once every four years, which is what makes them so uncommon.

It had become the tradition of the Silk family to celebrate Griffin's birthday on the twenty-eighth day of February, so it came as a surprise when he asked Nell if he could have a party on the twenty-seventh day of February.

"But the twenty-seventh is a Friday. Wouldn't it be better to have it on the weekend?" asked Nell. "We could have it on the Sunday, the first of March, if you really want a change."

But Griffin was determined. "Please, Nell, I really want to have it on the twenty-seventh," he pleaded, hoping his grandmother wouldn't guess why.

"I might need to take the day off school to help you," he said hopefully. But Nell just smiled and shook her head.

Layla offered to go home with him after school on the day of the party and help with the organizing. She was delighted when Griffin told her she was invited. "You'll have to dress up," he said. "Nell will loan you a hat and some high-heeled shoes if you want them."

Layla had brought a stamp and an envelope from home, and at lunchtime she helped Griffin write an invitation to his mother. "I'll mail it on the way home, and then it will be a secret," she said, and Griffin could tell that Layla liked secrets.

There are some days when heaven seems much closer to earth than others, and Friday the twenty-seventh of February was one of them. At dusk the sky was watermelon pink, furrowed with apricot. Sweet, sunbaked fruit still clung to the branches of the Cox's orange pippin and filled the thick, warm air with the smell of apple pie.

The Rainbow Girls loved parties and had helped Layla dress up in an old straw hat of Nell's with a peacock feather stuck in its crown and a pair of high-heeled red shoes. They loaned her long strands of glittering glass beads and an elegant pair of black evening gloves, which came right up to her armpits. Griffin wondered how they would feel when they found out the real reason for the party.

While Nell and the girls prepared the food and drink inside the house, Griffin and Layla scattered cushions like colored confetti on the grass. Blue, looking splendid in a red satin bow tie, sat down on the biggest of the cushions. Zeus perched on a bough of the apple tree preening his coal black feathers. Griffin wanted to put Mama's old cane chair under the tree, but he thought he would wait and see. He hadn't had a reply to his invitation, but Layla said it took a long time for letters to get all the way down to the city. He hoped it had arrived.

Daddy had promised not to be too late for the party, but already it was starting to get dark. Nell lit some portable gaslights and hung them from the branches of the tree, and Violet and Amber arranged terra-cotta pots with candles in them along the table. Just as Griffin and Layla got to the porch to wait for Daddy, Scarlet called out from inside the house and asked them to take some plates of food down to the table. By the time they had finished, Griffin could hear the familiar whine of his father's truck.

He stood still for a moment, almost afraid to go and look. Layla took his hand, and together they walked to the front of the house. As the truck neared, Daddy began to sound the horn. Nell and the Rainbow Girls came running to see what the fuss was all about, and as the truck wheeled to a stop in front of the shed, Griffin felt as though his feet had been nailed to the ground.

It was too dark to see inside the windows of the truck. Daddy jumped down from the cabin and ran around to the other door. He swung it open and leaned inside, and when he turned, there was Mama in his arms. The girls all rushed over to greet her.

"Gently, girls, gently," said Daddy, and he carefully let Mama down onto the rough gravel path of her home. She kissed them all and then hung on to Daddy's arm. And as she slowly walked toward Griffin and Layla, Griffin saw that she held in her hand the envelope he and Layla had sent her with the invitation inside it.

"Thank you, Griffin," she said softly, and knelt down to hold him close.

She held him with warm, strong, loving arms. This was Mama. Not the sad, frail stranger they had all visited at Christmas, who had looked through them, past them, as though she was trying to see someone else. This was Mama, almost as she had been before Tishkin went away.

"Thank you so much," she whispered, "for making me see that it was time I came home to my family."

She stood up then and said, "You must be Layla."

Griffin wondered how his mother knew Layla's

name. Layla nodded happily, and although she wasn't wearing a crown tonight, she extended her elegantly gloved hand.

"I'm so pleased to meet you, Layla," Mama went on, "and thank you very much for the little note you put in with the invitation."

Then Griffin realized how Mama knew Layla's name. Layla hadn't told him that she was going to put a note in his invitation. He wondered what she had written on it.

Naming Tishkin

Most special occasions in the Silk family were celebrated according to a pattern. And each celebration had its own pattern. Griffin found it comforting to know the way things would be. For birthday parties, the food was eaten before the present giving and speeches. Naming Day Ceremonies were different. First came the speeches and then the feasting. So Griffin knew that he had to start the Naming Day Ceremony right away.

He picked up his schoolbag and walked to the

end of the long table, where Daddy usually stood on Naming Days.

Layla said, "Shush, everybody."

And the breeze held its breath and the girls stilled their tongues and it seemed that the whole world waited, while Griffin took something from his bag with shaking fingers. It looked like a flower press. It was a flower press. It was the one Daddy had carved him for his third Christmas. There was silence as he unscrewed the brass wing nuts and removed the carved wooden top.

"I thought we should have a Naming Day for our baby sister," he said without lifting his eyes from the press in front of him. "That's why I wanted the party today, because it would have been her first birthday. I haven't got a proper Naming Day Book for her, but I thought we could use my flower press to start with, because that's where I put her daisy chain." He lifted the tissue from the first page, and underneath was the baby-size crown, pressed flat and kept perfect since Tishkin went away.

Griffin picked it up carefully, and it swung like a hoop of tiny suns from his finger. He looked up and saw the candlelight dancing in nine pairs of eyes as they waited for him to speak again, and all

the words that he wanted to say stuck to the roof of his mouth.

Daddy stood up and walked to the end of the table. He put his arm around Griffin's shoulders and said, "You're right, Griffin, we should have planned a Naming Day, but we've been too sad to do it. We've stopped talking about our baby, all of

us, because in some way each of us felt that there must have been something we could have done to stop her from dying, that in some way it was our fault."

Griffin looked up at his father, surprised. He hadn't known that other people felt like that too.

Daddy continued, "But there was nothing any of us could have done." For a while there was silence while images of the baby Silk floated before each one of them. "It has taken the courage of a lion to do what you have done today, Griffin," said Daddy. "You are right. Though your sister stayed with us such a short time, we must celebrate her life. We should offer her a name."

He had placed a brown paper parcel on the table and began to unwrap it. "I started to carve a cover for her book, but I put it away when she died." Griffin was surprised; he hadn't known about the book. It was a beautiful cover. There was a baby on it with plump cheeks and curly hair, and from her back sprouted two little wings, so that she looked like an angel. "When Mama got your invitation, there was a note inside from Layla. She said you had a special name that you call our baby. Mama and I talked about it on the way home, and we would like it very much if you would offer that name to our baby. Then I'll carve it on the cover."

Griffin looked down to where Mama sat in her cane chair under the gaslit apple boughs with her yellow hair streaming down her back and on her lips the most beautiful smile. Nell sat beside her in the grass, with Zeus perched on her shoulder, his white eye bright in the darkness. The lipstick smiles on the Rainbow Girls were as wide as clowns' mouths. At Griffin's bare, brown feet sat Blue, feeling the vibrations of his master's voice. And Layla, his friend, lay on her back, carefully watching the patches of moonlight between the gaps in the leaves. It was like a photograph in Griffin's head, one he knew he would never forget.

Just then a gentle breath of wind passed by the Kingdom of Silk and rustled the leaves of the Cox's orange pippin. Griffin heard them whisper, and he raised his mighty wings and lifted his head to the heavens and called out in a loud, clear voice, "To my little sister, I offer you the name of Tishkin Silk."